A jock and a brainiac making it to callbacks?

stamp

East High's very own Romeo and Juliet

stamp

Sharpay and Ryan—drama queen and king of EHS.

stamp

Chad and Taylor think athletes and "mathletes" don't mix, but Troy and Gabriella are about to prove them wrong!

stamp

HIGH SCHOOL MUSICAL

HIGH SCHOOL MUSICAL

HIGH SCHOOL MUSICAL

HIGH
SCHOOL
MUSICAL

© Disney

HIGH
SCHOOL
MUSICAL

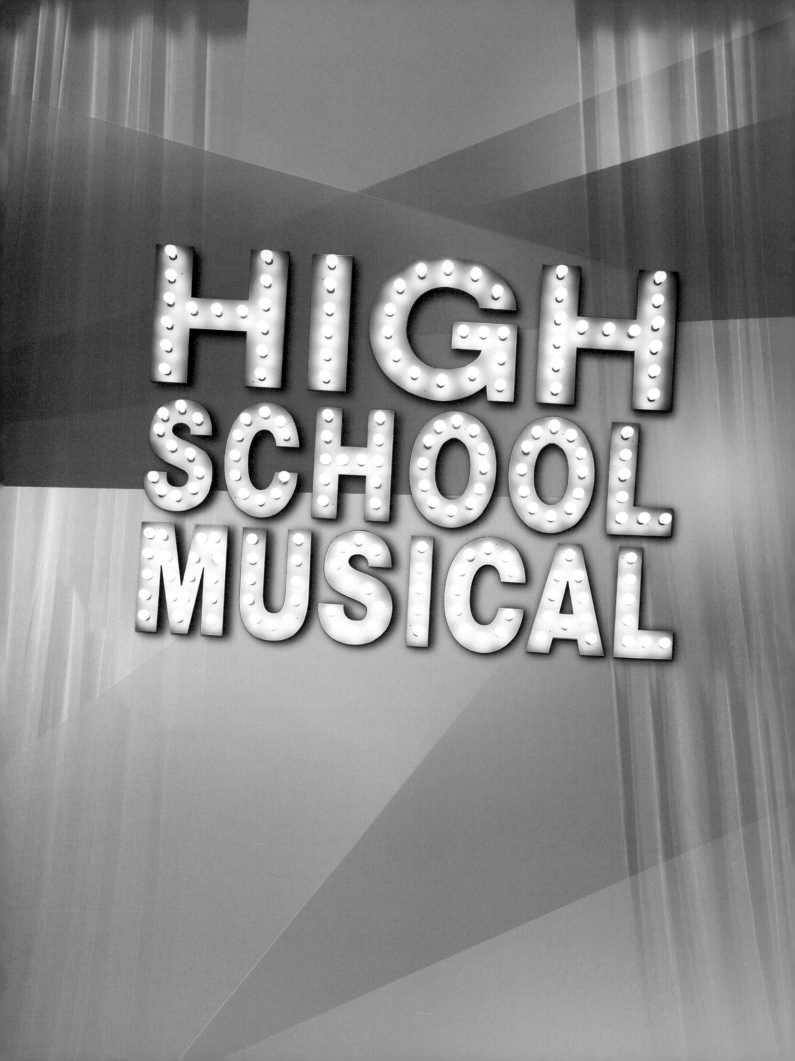

HIGH
SCHOOL
MUSICAL

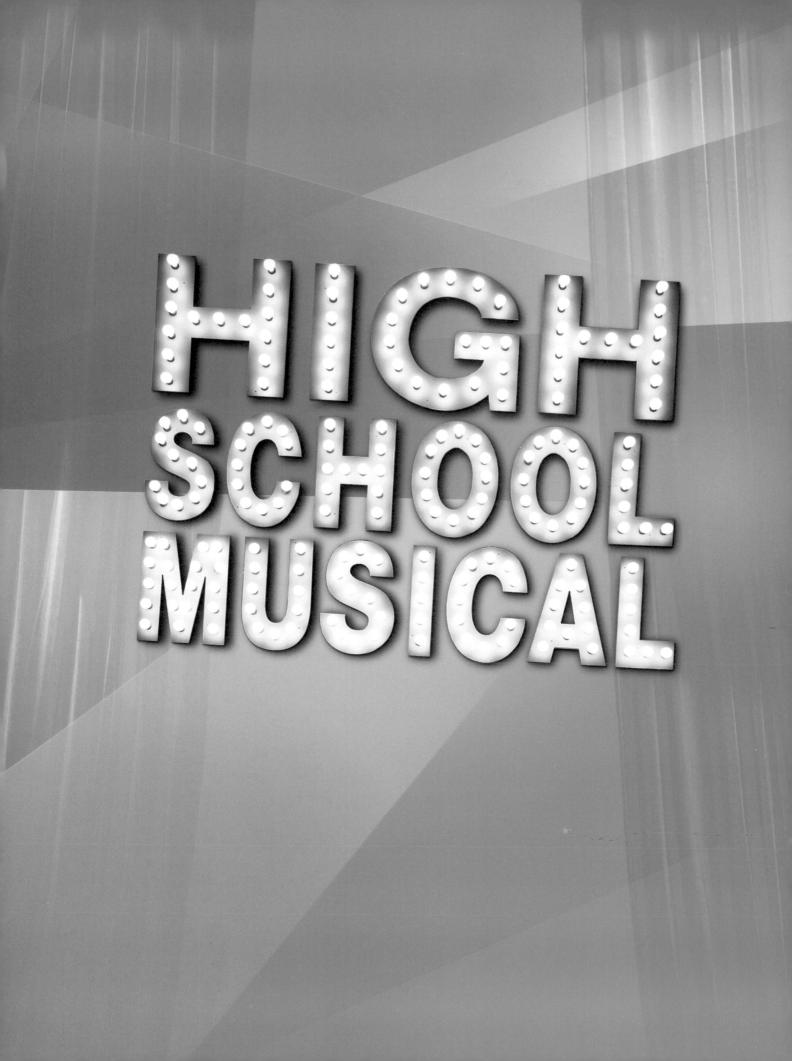

HIGH
SCHOOL
MUSICAL

HIGH SCHOOL MUSICAL

© Disney

HIGH SCHOOL MUSICAL

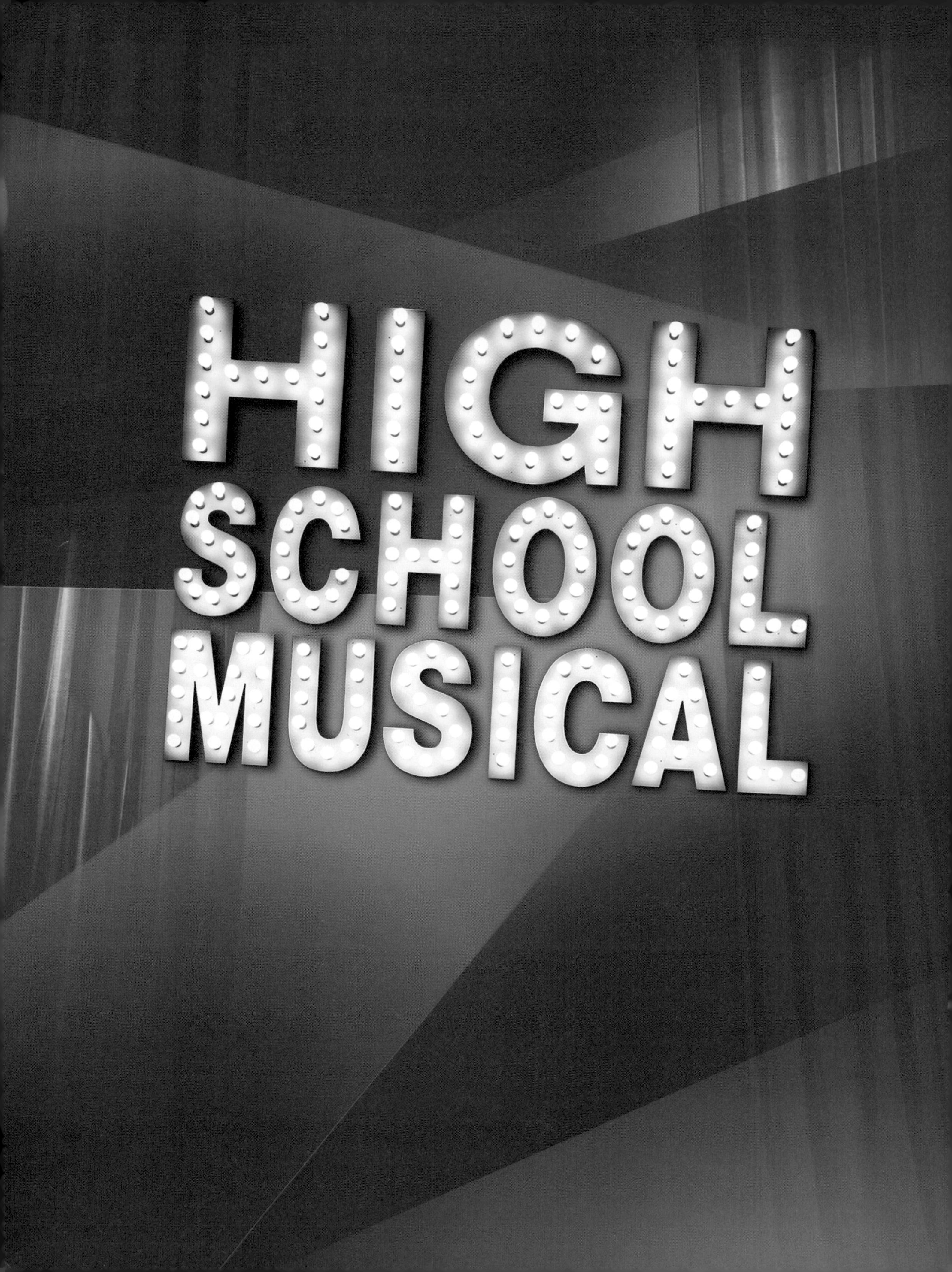
HIGH
SCHOOL
MUSICAL

The basketball team gets focused.

stamp

Chad thinks Troy should get his mind off music and concentrate on the championship.

stamp

The Wildcats celebrate winning the big game.

stamp

East High's star basketball player is a great dancer, too!

stamp